To parents and teachers

We hope you and the children will enjoy reading this story in English or Spanish. The story is simple, but not *simplified,* so that both versions are quite natural. However, there is lots of repetition for practicing pronunciation, for helping develop memory skills, and for reinforcing comprehension.

At the back of the book there is a small picture dictionary with the key words and a basic pronunciation guide to the whole story.

Here are a few suggestions for using the book:

• Read the story aloud in English first, to get to know it. Treat it like any other picture book: look at the pictures, talk about the story, the characters, and so on.

• Then look at the picture dictionary and say the key words in Spanish. Ask the children to say the words out loud, rather than reading them.

• Go back and read the story again, this time in English *and* Spanish. Don't worry if your pronunciation isn't quite correct. Just have fun trying it out. Check the guide at the back of the book, if necessary, but you'll soon pick up how to say the Spanish words.

• When you think you and the children are ready, try reading the story in Spanish only. Ask the children to say it with you. Only ask them to read it if they seem eager to try. The spelling could be confusing and discourage them.

• Above all encourage the children, and give lots of praise. Little children are usually quite unselfconscious and this is excellent for building up confidence in a foreign language.

First edition for the United States, its Dependencies, Canada, and the Philippines published 2000 by Barron's Educational Series, Inc.
Text © Copyright 2000 by b small publishing, Surrey, England.

International Standard Book Number 0-7641-5283-1   Library of Congress Catalog Card Number 00-131745
Printed in China   9 8 7 6 5 4 3

Puppy finds a friend

Cachorrito encuentra un amigo

Catherine Bruzzone

Pictures by John Bendall-Brunello
Spanish by Thessa Judkins

BARRON'S

Puppy wakes up.

Cachorrito se despierta.

It's Saturday.

Es sábado.

"Hmm…who can I play with today?"

"Mmm…¿con quién puedo jugar hoy?"

"I'm too tired," says the cat,

"Estoy demasiado cansado",
dice el gato,

"come back tomorrow."

"vuelve mañana".

"I'm too busy," says the cow,

"Estoy demasiado ocupada",
dice la vaca,

"come back later."

"vuelve más tarde".

"I'm too hungry," says the horse,

"Tengo demasiada hambre",
dice el caballo,

"come back this evening."

"vuelve esta tarde".

"I can't leave my nest," says the hen,

"No puedo dejar mi nido",
dice la gallina,

"come back on Monday."

"vuelve el lunes".

"Come and swim with us," say the ducks.

"Ven a nadar con nosotros",
dicen los patos.

But Puppy doesn't like water.

Pero a Cachorrito no le gusta el agua.

So he goes home.
Así que vuelve a su casa.

He plays with his ball.
Juega con su pelota.

He eats his lunch.
Come su almuerzo.

He sleeps in his basket.
Duerme en su canasta.

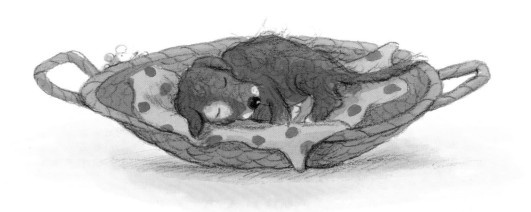

"Who's there?"

"¿Quién está allí?"

"Can I play with you, Puppy?"

"¿Puedo jugar contigo, Cachorrito?"

"Mouse, you're my best friend!"

"¡Ratón, eres mi mejor amigo!"

Pronouncing Spanish

Don't worry if your pronunciation isn't quite correct.
The important thing is to be willing to try.

The pronunciation guide is based on the Spanish accent used
in Latin America. Although it cannot be completely accurate,
it certainly will be a great help.

• Read the guide as naturally as possible, as if it were English.

• Put stress on the letters in *italics*, e.g. *ag*wah.

If you can, ask a Spanish-speaking person to help, and move
on as soon as possible to speaking the words without the guide.

Note: Spanish adjectives usually have two forms, one for masculine
and one for feminine nouns, e.g. **cansado** and **cansada** (see the
next page).

Words Las palabras

lass pal-*abrass*

cat
el gato

el *gat*-oh

duck
el pato

el *pah*-toh

hen
la gallina

lah gahl-*eenah*

horse
el caballo

el ka*bah*-yoh

cow
la vaca

la *b*akah

mouse
el ratón

l rat*on*

Puppy
Cachorrito

kachoh-*reetoh*

friend
el amigo/la amiga

el a*meegoh*/lah a*meegah*

basket
la canasta

lah ka*nah*-stah

nest
el nido

el *nee*doh

tired
cansado/
cansada

kan*sah*-doh/kan*sah*-dah

busy
ocupado/
ocupada

okoo*pah*-doh/okoo*pah*-dah

to be hungry
tener hambre

tenair *ambreh*

ball
la pelota
lah peh-*loh*-tah

lunch
el almuerzo
el alm*wair*so

water
el agua
el *agwah*

to swim
nadar
nad-*ar*

to play
jugar
hoo*gar*

to eat
comer
koh-mair

today
hoy
oy

this evening
esta tarde
estah tar-deh

tomorrow
mañana
man-*yah*-nah

Monday
lunes
looness

Saturday
sábado
sah-badoh

A simple guide to pronouncing this Spanish story

Cachorrito encuentra un amigo
kachoh-*reet*oh en*kwen*tra oon a*mee*goh

Cachorrito se despierta.
kachoh-*reet*oh seh despee*air*-tah

Es sábado.
ess *sah*-badoh

"Mmm...¿con quién puedo jugar hoy?"
mmm...kon kee-*en* p*way*doh
hoo*gar* oy

"Estoy demasiado cansado", dice el gato,
estoy demass-*yah*-doh kan*sah*-doh,
dee-seh el *gat*-oh

"vuelve mañana".
well-weh man-*yah*-nah

"Estoy demasiado ocupada", dice la vaca,
estoy demass-*yah*-doh okoo*pah*-dah,
dee-seh lah *bak*ah

"vuelve más tarde".
well-weh mass *tar*-deh

"Tengo demasiada hambre", dice el caballo,
tengo demass-*yah*-dah *am*breh,
dee-seh el ka*bah*-yoh

"vuelve esta tarde".
well-weh *es*tah *tar*-deh

"No puedo dejar mi nido", dice la gallina,
noh p*way*doh deh-*har* mee *nee*doh,
dee-seh lah gahl-*een*ah

"vuelve el lunes".
well-weh el *loon*ess

"Ven a nadar con nosotros", dicen los patos.
ben ah nad-*ar* kon no*ss*otross,
dee-sehn lohs *pah*-tohs

Pero a Cachorrito no le gusta el agua.
pair*oh* ah kachoh-*reet*oh noh leh *goo*stah
el *ag*wah

Así que vuelve a su casa.
as*see* keh *well*-weh ah soo *kas*ah

Juega con su pelota.
hw*ay*gah kon soo peh-*loh*-tah

Come su almuerzo.
koh-meh soo almw*air*so

Duerme en su canasta.
dw*air*meh en soo ka*nah*-stah

"¿Quién está allí?"
kee-*en* ess-*tah* ah-*yee*

"¿Puedo jugar contigo, Cachorrito?"
p*way*doh hoo*gar* kon*tee*-goh kachoh-*reet*oh

"¡Ratón, eres mi mejor amigo!"
rat*on* *air*ess mee meh-*hor* a*mee*goh